THE PUPPY PLACE

CHAMP

THE PUPPY PLACE

**Don't miss any of these
other stories by Ellen Miles!**

THE PUPPY PLACE

CHAMP

ELLEN MILES

SCHOLASTIC INC.

For K-9 teams everywhere, with much gratitude for all they do

Copyright © 2016 by Ellen Miles
Cover art by Tim O'Brien
Original cover design by Steve Scott

ISBN 978-0-545-85727-7

10 9 8 7 6 5 4 3   16 17 18 19 20

Printed in the U.S.A.   40
First printing 2016

CHAPTER ONE

"No batter, no batter!"

Charles Peterson glared at the guy sitting next to him in the stands. Why was he yelling that? The man standing at the plate, waving a bat around as he waited for a pitch, happened to be Charles's father. Dad might not be the best softball player in the world, but Charles knew that he could hit: they played all the time in the backyard and even went to the batting cages together sometimes. "Home run, Dad!" he shouted over the guy's heckling. "Go for it!"

The man next to Charles grinned and shrugged.

"All in good fun," he said. "My brother's a cop, so I have to root for them."

The softball game was an annual spring event in Littleton: firefighters against police. Charles went every year, and of course he always rooted for the firefighters, since his dad was part of the Littleton Fire Department.

Unfortunately, the firefighters always lost.

So far.

Maybe, thought Charles, *this would be their year*. "My dad's a firefighter," he told the man.

The man nodded. "Good for him," he said. "And hey, it looks like they have a chance this time."

It was true. They were in the top of the ninth inning, and the police still had not scored a run. The firefighters hadn't, either, but now they had two runners on base. Charles knew them both: Meg was on first, and Rick, one of the newer guys on the squad, was on third. "Bring 'em home, Dad,"

Charles yelled as the pitcher wound up. He knew that the police would still have a chance to score when they came up at the end of the inning, but a couple of runs would be great insurance.

"Yup," said the man as the ball sailed over the plate, "they've got a chance, as long as Reggie doesn't show up."

"Steeerike!" yelled the ump.

Charles's dad stepped back from the plate, frowning and shaking his head.

"Reggie?" Charles asked. "Oh, right. Reggie. The guy who gets all the home runs." Now he remembered. Reggie was the main reason the police won every year. He was a state trooper, big and muscular. He could hit to just about any spot in the field, and he could field, too. He usually played third base. Sure enough, Charles saw that there was a new guy at third, an unfamiliar face. Definitely not Reggie. That was good news.

Charles's dad stepped back in, took his stance, and got ready for the next pitch. Charles had a feeling he was going to swing hard this time — but he didn't. The pitch came in low, and the umpire called, "Ball!"

"One and one," said the man next to Charles.

The next pitch was way to the outside. "Ball two," called the ump.

Charles's dad swung hard at the next pitch but didn't make contact. He kicked the dirt. Charles could tell he was frustrated. Another pitch, high and inside, and the count was full. "Come on, Dad," Charles said under his breath. "Come on!"

The pitcher wound up. She let the ball fly. Charles's dad stepped in, swung hard, and connected! The ball went sailing deep into left field. Charles jumped to his feet. "Yes!" he yelled when he saw the ball bounce to the ground between the two guys who'd been running for it. "Go, Dad!" he shouted as he watched his dad sprint for first. Already Rick had crossed home plate. Now Meg was between third and home, and Dad was rounding second. Out in left field, a player swept the ball up in his glove, bobbled it, recovered, and threw to the third baseman.

The throw was too hard, and the ball tipped off the third baseman's glove. "Go! Go! Go!" yelled Charles as Dad flew toward home. "Yesss!" Charles shouted as Dad slid across the plate. "Three runs! Go, Dad!" Dad looked up at him and grinned, holding his fists over his head.

Charles couldn't believe Mom had missed seeing this: she was at the nearby playground with Charles's little brother, the Bean. And Charles's sister, Lizzie, hadn't even come to the game. Well, they'd all be hearing about it at dinner that night, for sure.

The guy next to Charles was grinning, too.

"Nice hit," he said. He gave Charles a high five. "Your dad's a good player."

Charles nodded. He was proud of his father — for that three-run homer, and for a lot of other things, too. It was cool that he was a firefighter and an EMT: he helped people all the time. Dad was smart and funny and kind, and — Charles smiled — he loved puppies. If only everybody could see the way his dad cooed over little puppies.

Charles had seen his dad with a lot of puppies, since the Petersons were a foster family. That meant they took care of puppies who needed homes, just until they found each one the perfect forever family. Charles loved fostering, even though it was always hard to give the puppies up when the time came. He fell in love with each one and would have loved to keep them all. Fortunately, his family had kept one — the cutest, smartest, sweetest puppy ever. His name was Buddy. Buddy had soft brown fur and sparkly brown eyes. He wasn't any particular breed, but he wasn't "just a mutt." He was Charles's best friend in the whole world, and Charles told him everything.

Right then, Charles couldn't wait to tell Buddy about Dad's home run. "There was no way the police were going to come back after that," he would say as he scratched the heart-shaped white spot on his puppy's chest. "After Dad's hit, I knew that the firefighters were going to win this time."

"Uh-oh," said the man next to Charles. "Looks like your team's good luck might be about to come to an end." He pointed toward the parking lot near the police team dugout.

Charles looked — and groaned. It was Reggie, the big home-run hitter. But wait. What was that? A dark shadow flitted around Reggie's legs, following him as he strode toward his teammates. The police were coming off the field after their pitcher had caught a high pop-up for the last out. They cheered and laughed when they spotted Reggie, and the shadow shrank behind the big man.

The man next to Charles stood up for a better look. "What's Reggie doing with that scrawny puppy?" he asked.

CHAPTER TWO

"A puppy?" Charles stared at the man next to him. Then he turned to peer down at the shadow next to Reggie. Ever since he'd gotten glasses, Charles was amazed at what he could see. Like now: he saw a big head with a pointed nose and ears that stood up and a long, feathered tail. The man was right. That was definitely a dog. *A German shepherd*, Charles thought. Only this one wasn't the usual black and tan, like Scout, a shepherd the Petersons had once fostered. This one was pure black.

Charles stood up and began to pick his way down the bleachers. He had to get closer to that puppy. "Excuse me," he said as he stepped next to people's hands or backpacks. "Excuse me."

The closer he got, the more Charles saw. He saw that the black coat was matted and dull, not soft and shiny like Buddy's. He saw the dog's ribs sticking out, every bone visible. He saw two hip bones jutting up near the dog's tangled tail, and long skinny legs that made the puppy look like a newborn foal.

This young dog was in trouble.

Charles also saw the way the dog looked up at Reggie. The dog's tongue lolled out a little in a near smile and his eyes sparkled. Obviously, the dog loved Reggie. But was Reggie taking good care of the puppy? How could he have let him get so skinny?

He saw Dad approaching Reggie, too — of course. Dad couldn't stay away from a puppy, either. "Great hit!" Charles said, giving his dad a quick high five before turning his attention back to the dog.

"Thanks," Dad said. He knelt next to the rangy, scruffy pup, petting the dog's ears. "Let him smell you before you try to pet him."

Duh. Charles knew how to behave around a dog he didn't know. He knew to move closer very slowly and always let the dog come up to him. He held out his hand, palm down, so that the dog could stretch his neck forward and sniff it.

Sure enough, the dog took a few steps toward Charles, stretched out his neck, and sniffed very carefully and for quite a long time. Finally, he looked up and met Charles's eyes.

You're okay. I can tell you're not going to hurt me or my friend.

"When did you get a dog, Reggie?" asked Dad. Charles saw his eyes run over the dog's scrawny body and knew that his father was also wondering if Reggie was the right owner for this pup.

"Oh, he's not mine," Reggie said. "I found him last week, when I was working on a raid with the ASPCA. A place way up north, a farmhouse where the people kept over forty dogs and maybe a hundred cats. A few other assorted animals, too. Goats and rabbits and a horse. All of them were just about starving."

Charles stared at Reggie. "What? That's horrible!"

Reggie nodded. "It's called hoarding. The people who do it don't mean to hurt animals. They have sort of a mental illness that makes them want more and more animals, so they take them in — but then they can't afford to feed the animals or care for them when they get sick."

"Awful." Dad shook his head. "That's just awful. And this dog was one of them?"

Reggie nodded. "When we broke into the house, he was very protective of the other animals. He didn't growl or bark or anything. He just stood there in front of all the other animals, staring at us. Some of the animal control people thought they might be attacked if they tried to get past him. I managed to get him out of the way, into my patrol car."

"Weren't you scared?" Charles asked. "That he'd bite you, I mean?"

"I had German shepherds when I was a kid," said Reggie with a shrug. "I understand them. I could tell this guy wasn't vicious at all. He's a sweetheart, really. And he's all about taking care of others. Let me tell you, there were a lot of skinny dogs there, but he was the skinniest. One of the biggest, too. If he'd wanted to, he could have hogged whatever food they did get — but obviously he let some of the other, weaker dogs eat before he did."

The dog looked up at Reggie, sat down, and held up one paw. "See?" said Reggie. "He just wants to please me, and he's only known me for a few days. He's still got his spirit, even after everything he's been through. I'm going to hate to give him up."

"Are you taking him to Caring Paws?" asked Charles. That was the animal shelter where his sister volunteered every week.

Reggie shook his head. "None of the shelters have room right now. They're flooded with the animals from the raid, and the last thing they need is a dog who is overly protective. But I can't keep him, either. My landlady doesn't allow pets."

"Hey, Reggie!" yelled a guy from the police team. "Are you ready to play, or what? We need ya."

Reggie looked down at Charles. "What do you

think?" he asked. "Want to hold the puppy for me? I've heard that your family takes care of dogs."

Dad spoke up. "Is that why you brought him here? Were you going to ask us to foster him?"

Reggie looked down and kicked at the dirt. "Well, I —"

"We'll do it!" said Charles. He held out his hand for the leash, sure that his dad would agree.

"I don't know," said Dad. "This pup looks like he needs some special care."

"Dad, that's exactly why we have to help him," Charles said. "Please?"

"Yeah, please?" asked Reggie. "He does need some attention. But from what I hear, you're just the family to give it to him."

"Reggie!" yelled his teammates. "Ready to play?"

"Can I at least just hold him while Reggie plays?" Charles begged his father. "That will give us some time to think it over."

Charles's dad frowned. The dog sat back on his haunches and gazed up hopefully.

"Peterson!" someone yelled from the field. "Let's get going."

"Are you sure he's okay with children?" Dad asked Reggie.

"Positive," said Reggie. "He's been nothing but a gentleman with my neighbor's kids and my own niece and nephews."

Dad nodded. Then he turned to Charles. "Okay. Take him over to the end of the bleachers, where nobody else is sitting. And be careful."

Charles nodded happily. "He'll be safe with me."

Reggie and Dad trotted off toward the field. "Hey," Charles yelled to Reggie. "What's his name, anyway?"

CHAPTER THREE

"I've been calling him Champ," Reggie yelled over his shoulder as he headed toward his team's bench. He picked up three bats, holding them easily in his big hands as he stepped toward the on-deck area, where another batter was warming up. He swung them all together, then put down two of them and took some quicker cuts with the third. He was focused on what he was doing and didn't even glance back at Charles and the dog.

"Champ," Charles repeated. He liked the sound of that name, even if the scrawny dog did not exactly look like a champion.

The dog snapped to attention, gazing up at Charles with his intense golden-brown eyes.

Yes? What can I do? Do you need help with something?

"Wow," said Charles. "You've already learned your name. What a smartie." He dug into the pocket of his hoodie, hoping to find a dog treat. He usually carried a biscuit or two, at least, in case he met a dog. Yes! Half a biscuit was buried in the bottom corner along with some gray fuzz. "Hope you're not fussy," he said to Champ.

Charles didn't just hand the treat over. He knew that it was always good to expect a dog to do something for a treat: sit, come, lie down. "Don't give treats away for free," his sister, Lizzie, always said. "Every treat is a good opportunity for training." Lizzie was the best dog trainer in the family, because she read every book she could find on the subject.

"Champ, sit," Charles said. The dog was still looking up into his eyes, another great sign. "A dog who looks you in the eye is a dog who wants to please you" was another of Lizzie's sayings.

But Champ did not sit. Champ just stood there. Maybe he wasn't so smart after all.

"Sit," Charles said again. He couldn't resist, even though Lizzie always said that you should give each command only once before showing the dog what you wanted.

Champ stood still. He held up one front paw, still gazing into Charles's eyes.

I know you want me to do something — but I'm just not sure what it is!

"Oh," said Charles. "Oh, of course. How could you know how to sit? If your owners had forty dogs, they probably didn't have much time for training." He held the treat up, straight over Champ's nose, and moved it slowly backward. Champ turned his face up to watch the treat move, and almost automatically his hind end came down on the ground.

"Yes!" Charles said. That was one trick he knew how to teach, mainly because it was the easiest. "Good sit. What a good dog." He showed Champ the treat, and the dog reached out and took it. His mouth was as gentle as the touch of a butterfly wing. He didn't snap at the treat, like some dogs did, but he crunched it up eagerly. Charles could imagine how hungry Champ must be. He looked like he had not eaten a good meal in a long time.

Charles scratched him between the ears. "Good dog," he repeated. "Want to come stay with us for a while? We'll take good care of you."

Champ leaned against Charles's leg and let out a contented sigh.

It's been a long time since I had any attention. Keep scratching! That feels so good.

Charles looked down at the skinny dog. Poor thing. He was as starved for affection as he was for food. Charles loved dogs more than anything, but he could not imagine having forty. How could you even keep track of them? Dogs needed lots of attention and love. This dog especially.

Champ gazed up at Charles and leaned in even closer. Charles felt his heart swell. This was one special dog; he could tell that already.

Suddenly, the crowd in the bleachers erupted into cheers. Charles had been so busy getting to know Champ that he had completely forgotten about the softball game, but now he looked up just in time to see Reggie circling the bases as fielders chased after a ball he'd hit far into right field. Three other runners tagged up at home before Reggie crossed the plate. A grand slam! Reggie's teammates poured off the bench and ran to him for high fives and back-slapping hugs. The game was over, and the police had won again.

Charles grinned down at Champ. "Oops," he said. "I guess it's all my fault. If I hadn't agreed to hold you, Reggie couldn't have made that hit."

Dad trotted in from the field and joined Charles and Champ.

"Sorry, Dad," said Charles.

Dad shrugged. "It's just a game," he said. "And

win or lose, we still get to eat hot dogs and ice cream."

Hot dogs! Charles felt his stomach rumble with sudden hunger. How could he have forgotten all about the picnic after the game? That was the best part. Mom and the Bean would be back from the playground any minute. They could all eat together, and with a little bit of luck, Charles would be able to talk Mom into fostering Champ.

CHAPTER FOUR

Charles stood behind the backstop talking to Dad, with Champ leaning against his leg. Then Reggie trotted over, still pink-faced and panting from running the bases. Champ stood up straight and pulled on the leash, his ears up and his mouth slightly open in a doggy grin. "Champ," Charles said. "Easy, boy." But the dog was completely focused on Reggie.

"Hey, bud," said Reggie, stooping to pet Champ. "How did you like that homer?"

The scrawny black pup stretched up his neck to lick Reggie's cheek. His tail wagged hard.

You're back! I'm so glad to see you again!

Reggie laughed. "It's nice to have a fan waiting on the sidelines," he said, grinning at Charles.

"Great hit," said Charles.

"Yeah, nice one," said Dad, giving Reggie a high five. "Even if you did steal our lead — and the game."

"Thanks," said Reggie. "I might have only played one inning, but I feel about as hungry as this guy looks." He gave Champ a scratch between the ears. "I think both of us could use a hot dog."

"Better go slow on the people food," Dad said. "If he hasn't eaten much for a while, it might be too rich for his stomach."

Reggie nodded. "Good point. See? You people know about dogs. That's why I came to you."

They headed for the picnic tables that sat under some nearby trees. Charles saw bowls of potato salad and coleslaw and plates of deviled eggs. Platters of hot dogs and hamburgers were already coming from the grill. It was a good thing some of the firefighters and police liked cooking more than playing softball. They always put on an awesome feast. Still, Charles hung back a bit, holding Champ on his leash. He didn't want the dog to feel overwhelmed by all the people and the food smells. He found a table where nobody was sitting and perched on the bench.

"Mom!" Charles stood up when he saw his mom approaching with the Bean. He waved her over. "You have to come meet Champ."

Mom raised her eyebrows in surprise when she saw the dog at the end of the leash. "Where did he come from?" she asked. "And . . . is he okay with little kids?"

"Reggie says that he is," said Charles. "The Bean knows what to do. Let's give them a chance to meet."

"Uppy!" yelled the Bean, tugging Mom's hand. The Bean had never met a dog he didn't love.

"Slowly," said Mom. "Remember, let him sniff your hand and get to know you."

Before long, Champ and the Bean were exchanging kisses. Charles could see that the skinny puppy was as gentle as a mother dog. Champ wagged his tail and nuzzled the Bean's cheeks while the Bean petted him. Charles told his mom all about where Champ had come from and why Reggie needed their help.

"Isn't he beautiful?" Charles asked his mom.

"Well . . ." Mom gave the scrawny black pup a doubtful look.

"I know he's a little thin, but look at his head. He's so handsome," said Charles. He petted Champ as he watched Reggie dig into the food, and his mouth watered. Suddenly, he couldn't wait for a hot dog.

Mom seemed to read his mind. She held out her hand for the leash. "Go ahead, get some food," she said. "I'll keep an eye on Champ."

Charles grinned. He had a feeling Mom was going to say yes to fostering Champ. "I'll bring you a plate, too," he said.

At the food table, police and firefighters were joking with each other about the game as they loaded their plates. "We almost had you," Dad said to one of the state troopers, a big man with a big smile.

"Not even close," the man teased back.

"Come sit with us, Sarge," Dad said. "Charles, this is Sergeant McCloskey. He's in charge of all the K-9 units in the state. You know, the police who have dogs for partners?"

"I met Thor once," Charles said. "Do you know him?" Charles had never forgotten the time a K-9 officer had brought his dog to school for a demonstration.

"Thor is an excellent dog," Sarge said as they walked to the Petersons' table with loaded plates. "Too bad he and Officer Frost transferred to a police force in Montana. We miss them."

Charles's eyes lit up. "So you need a dog to replace him," he said. "Wait till you meet Champ."

"He's one of the dogs from the hoarding case," Dad explained. "A shepherd. We may be fostering him."

But when Sarge sat down next to Reggie and saw Champ lying on the ground near the trooper's feet, he laughed. "That scrawny thing? He'd never make it through the training," he said.

"Maybe he'll make a good pet for somebody, but he's not cut out for police work."

Charles was disappointed, and he saw that Reggie looked a little hurt.

Dad must have noticed, too. He changed the subject quickly. "Well, you guys might have beat us at softball today, but we'll get you back when we win the raft race."

The raft race! Charles perked up. That was the next big event of the spring. The raft race happened every year, when the river was running at its highest. Each team made its own wacky raft out of scrap materials. They were almost more like parade floats, with themes and costumes. The past year, the winner had a Star Trek theme, with a raft that was supposed to look like the *Enterprise*. Some of the rafts sank, some ended up going down the river backward or sideways, and a few reached the finish line to huge cheers and major bragging rights.

Charles and his friends David and Sammy had already been talking about the raft race. Kids couldn't pilot rafts, but they could help build them and they could ride on them as crew — and Charles had an idea for a fantastic theme. He couldn't wait to tell Dad.

Sarge picked up his hot dog and took a big bite. "The raft race? Sure!" he said. "You're on."

Later, on the way home, Charles sat in the backseat with Champ leaning against him. Champ had not wanted to leave Reggie, but now that he was in the Petersons' van, he seemed content. Charles leaned back against Champ. He was sleepy after eating three hot dogs and mounds of potato salad. "Wait till we get home," Charles murmured to the dog. "You and Buddy are going to get along great. And we'll feed you so your ribs don't stick out anymore."

Champ leaned in closer and licked Charles's ear.

I know I can trust you. Something tells me I'm a very lucky dog!

CHAPTER FIVE

"Aye, me hearties!" yelled Sammy as he tossed a big piece of lumber onto the "keep" pile.

Charles shook his head and laughed. "We're going to be Vikings, not pirates," he reminded his friend.

"Vikings," said David. "They were the guys with those hats — the ones with the big horns on them, right?"

David and Sammy had come over to help build a raft — the raft Charles hoped would win the race. It was going to be so cool: a Viking ship with a big, high prow (that was what you called the front part of a ship, Charles had discovered) and

Viking flags flying from the mast. Since Dad would be the pilot, their victory would be a victory for the firefighters.

Now Charles nodded at his friend. "Right, the Vikings," he said. "Remember when we read about them in class? They were amazing sailors. They probably discovered America a long time before Christopher Columbus did!"

Dad nodded. "That's right," he said. "And David's right about the horns. We should wear those hats when we sail the raft. I bet I can find some at the costume shop." He gave up trying to unscrew a large rusty bolt and picked up his hammer to bang on it instead.

They were taking apart the old wooden swing set in the Petersons' backyard. Charles and Lizzie hardly ever used it anymore. It was babyish, with a silly short slide, tiny monkey bars, and two small swings. Even the Bean was bored with it, and anyway, it was starting to fall apart. "I've been meaning to take this thing down for a year now," Dad said, wiping his forehead with the back of his hand.

"It'll be perfect wood for our Viking ship," said Charles. "And then we can build something new back here — maybe a tree house?" He looked at Buddy, sleeping in the shade near the fence. "A low tree house, with stairs that a puppy can get up," he added. He squatted down to pet Champ, who lay nearby. Champ was not snoozing like Buddy was, even though they had played happily all morning, zooming around the yard. He was alert; he lay with his paws in front of him, watching everything that was happening with his intelligent golden-brown eyes.

Champ was different from any other puppy the Petersons had fostered. He was older than many of them — Lizzie had guessed that he might be about a year old — so maybe that was part of it. He seemed thoughtful and wise; he paid attention to what was going on around him. He was kind, too. That morning, when Charles had fed both dogs, Champ had waited for Buddy to finish eating before he stepped forward to clean his own bowl. "See? Reggie was right," Charles had said to Dad as they watched. "He's so skinny because he made sure all the other dogs ate first."

Now Champ lay there keeping an eye on Charles and his friends as they clambered over the swing set, helping sort the lumber, while Dad used a wrench to undo the big bolts that held the slide together.

"Remember when I fell off this swing?" Charles asked. He pulled the swing toward him and let it go, watching it glide. "I loved to pump as hard as I could and go really high."

"Of course I remember." Dad stood up and put his hands on his back, sighing as he stretched. "That was your first-ever trip to the emergency room. Luckily, you didn't need stitches for that cut on your leg."

"I got stitches once." Sammy pointed to his chin. "See? I still have the scar. It's from when I tripped over my Lego castle."

David pointed to his head. "Remember these stitches?" he asked. "From when I fell while when we were playing circus with Sweetie?"

Charles groaned. "That was scary," he said. Sweetie was a smart, funny miniature poodle that his family had fostered, and he and David and Sammy had thought she would make a perfect circus dog. They were practicing a human pyramid when Sweetie spotted Slinky, David's cat, and the whole thing tumbled down. Charles had not known that so much blood could gush out of someone's head.

"Okay," said Dad. "Enough talk about injuries. Let's take this slide down and walk it over to the side of the house. I'll haul it to the recycling center later this week."

The boys helped lift the slide and lug it across the yard. Champ got up and followed them, watching carefully. Charles had the feeling that if Champ could speak, he'd be saying, "Careful, now. Oops, step a little to the right. Watch out for that tree! Okay, that's good."

"Great," said Dad, brushing off his hands. "Next, the monkey bars."

They went back to the swing set, with Champ trotting along beside them. Dad got to work on one of the big bolts that attached the monkey bars to the swing set frame. "Ugh," he said. "This one's so tight even the hammer won't work. I'm going to have to spray on some oil before I can loosen it. I've got some in the basement."

He glanced up at the monkey bars. "Stay off those until I come back," he said as he set down his wrench and headed for the house.

Charles rolled his eyes. "After I fell off the swing, he and my mom were always so worried about me," he told his friends. "I wasn't supposed to go on the monkey bars when I was alone." He hopped up to try to grab a bar so he could pull himself along one last time before the bars came down. He missed, hopped again, and missed again. "Sometimes my parents still think I'm four," he said. He hopped one more time, and this time he caught a bar.

Crack!

It broke apart the minute his weight was on it,

sending him tumbling to the ground. David and Sammy started to laugh, but they stopped when Charles began to moan.

"My leg," he said, grabbing his ankle. "Ow!"

He rolled onto his side and looked around to see if his dad was on his way back out to the yard, but all he saw was Champ, dashing toward the house.

CHAPTER SIX

Charles lay beneath the monkey bars, holding his leg. He couldn't believe how much it hurt. There was no point in even trying to stand up; he knew there was no way his leg could hold his weight. "Ohhh," he moaned.

"Are you okay?" David asked.

"Noooo," Charles moaned.

Champ had dashed up the deck stairs. Now he stood at the back door, barking in short, loud bursts.

Hey! We need help out here! Someone's hurt!

After a moment, the door swung open. "What in the —" Charles saw his dad stare down at the barking dog, then shift his gaze to the backyard. "Oh!" he said. He ran down the steps and straight to Charles's side. "What happened?" he asked as he squatted down. "Is it just your leg? Did you hit your head?"

There were too many questions, and answering them seemed way too complicated. Charles just moaned.

"He was trying to get on the monkey bars," said Sammy. "I mean, he did get on that one." He pointed. "But it broke."

"Which is why I told him to stay off it," Dad said. "I saw that it was rotted and about to go."

"Sorry, Dad," Charles said, finally getting some real words out. "It's just my leg, not my head."

"Oh, honey," Dad said. "It's okay." He touched Charles's thigh. "Up here?" he asked.

"No, my ankle," said Charles. He felt his dad's gentle touch on the place where it hurt. "There!" said Charles. "Oh, it hurts!"

Dad took his hand away. "I'm just glad Champ let us know right away."

"Champ," Charles said. "Where's Champ?" The dog stepped forward from behind Dad and nuzzled Charles's cheek. "Thanks, Champ," said Charles.

"Charles?" Mom burst out the back door. "Charles, are you all right?"

"It's his ankle," Dad said. "I'll drive him to the ER."

"No, the ambulance will. I'm calling 911," said Mom. She disappeared into the house before Dad could say a word.

Dad touched Charles's head again. "You're sure you didn't hit your head?"

Charles nodded, biting his lip. His ankle was

really throbbing now. "But I can't stand up," he said.

"Don't worry about that," Dad said. He squatted down, close to Charles. "Put your arms around my neck," he directed. "We'll have you out in front when the ambulance comes. Now, one . . . two . . . three, here we go!" He hoisted Charles up, carrying him like a little baby. Charles would have been embarrassed, but his leg hurt so much that he didn't care how it looked. "Okay?" Dad asked.

Charles nodded. The motion had made pain shoot through his ankle, but now it was back to throbbing. "Can Champ come with us?" he asked.

Dad smiled. "I don't think they'll let him into the emergency room," he said. "But maybe David and Sammy can stay with him and make sure he's all right. Are your parents home, Sammy?"

Sammy nodded. "They're working in the garden. I can see them." Sammy lived next door.

"Good," Dad said. "Can you take Champ with you and take care of him until you hear from us?"

Sammy nodded again. "Definitely, Mr. Peterson. You can count on us."

Charles almost had to laugh at how mature Sammy sounded, but instead he just groaned. "Thanks," he managed to say as he waved good-bye to his friends over Dad's shoulder. "Bye, Champ!"

Dad took a few slow steps. "How are you doing?" he asked Charles. "Okay?"

Charles nodded. He knew Dad was trying his best to move smoothly, but every step still jarred his leg. "Tell Champ it's all right," he called to his friends. "He looks worried."

Champ was trotting obediently along next to Sammy and David, but he kept gazing back at Charles. His brow was wrinkled and his ears were down. He let out a soft whimper.

Is everything okay? Are you going to be all right?

"Don't worry, pal," Dad told the dog. "He'll get the best of care. That's a promise."

As they moved around to the front of the house, Charles could hear the wail of a siren. The ambulance was on its way! It pulled up with a final burp of its siren, and two guys jumped out. Charles knew them, since they worked with his dad. In fact, they were the same guys who had shown up the time David hurt his head, Andy and Scott. They checked Charles out while they asked Dad a series of rapid-fire questions.

"I'll be there as soon as I find someone to watch the Bean," Mom said as the men lifted Charles into a cot inside the ambulance. She watched as they settled him in; then she waved. "I'll be right there," she said again as the doors closed.

Dad climbed into the ambulance with Charles and kept up a steady stream of talking as they drove off. The siren screamed and the ambulance roared along, speeding faster than any car Charles had ever been in. It was exciting, but he couldn't really enjoy it, since his leg hurt so much. "Almost there," Dad said. "We're just about to pull into the ER entrance. Hang in there, pal."

Moments later, Charles felt the ambulance take a turn, then come to a stop. Two nurses were waiting with a wheelchair when the ambulance doors opened. Dad seemed to know both of them. "Hey," he said. "Thanks for the royal treatment."

"I'm Sheryl," one of the nurses said to Charles as she helped Andy and Scott lift him out of the ambulance and into the wheelchair. "Sunny and I are here to help. Don't you worry about a thing." They wheeled him down a hall and got him settled on a hospital bed in one of the curtained treatment areas. Sunny put a bag of ice on his ankle while Sheryl interviewed Dad about what had happened and wrote down a million things about how old Charles was and how much he weighed and when he had last eaten and what he had last eaten. Charles was glad his dad was answering her questions, because he felt pretty woozy.

After that, stuff just kept happening, and Charles sort of lost track. A doctor came in — Dad knew her, too — and gently touched Charles's leg while she asked even more questions. She and one of the nurses put Charles's ankle into a splint, a stiff cardboard cuff that held his ankle steady. Then she gave him a pill to take. "This will help with the pain while you're getting X-rayed," she said. "We need to find out exactly what's going on inside there." Another nurse came to wheel him down a long hall and into a quiet green room, where another person helped him lie on a table while they took X-rays of his ankle. After that, there was more waiting, and the nurses made jokes with Dad, and Mom showed up, and people kept coming in and going out, and Charles finally gave up trying to keep track and closed his eyes.

He just wanted to be home. He wanted his leg to stop hurting. He wanted to be with Buddy and Champ, and he wanted everything to be normal and all this just to be a bad dream. But when he opened his eyes, the doctor was talking to Mom and Dad. "It's not a terrible fracture," she was saying. "But he'll definitely have to have a cast on that ankle."

CHAPTER SEVEN

It wasn't a dream. Charles really had broken his ankle (the doctor said that it was something called a hairline fracture), and he really did have to have a cast — but not yet. Before she put on his real cast, the doctor wanted to wait for the swelling to go down, so Charles went home in a special splint that kept his ankle steady.

"You mean we can't sign it?" asked David when he and Sammy came over the next day.

Charles shook his head. "They're just going to take this one off in a day or two," he said. He was lying on a lounge chair on the deck with his foot propped up on a pillow, a glass of lemonade on the table next to him, and Buddy and Champ lying nearby. Mom had settled him there so he could watch as his friends helped Dad work on the raft.

"More lemonade, Charles?" Mom asked, poking her head out the back door. "Oh, hi, boys. Would you like some lemonade, too? And Lizzie made some cookies for Charles. I'm sure he'll share."

Sammy raised his eyebrows. "Nice treatment," he said.

"I know," said Charles. "Plus, I got to choose anything I wanted for dinner last night, and I got to pick the movie we watched." Unfortunately, he had not really felt hungry, even for Chinese takeout, and he had fallen asleep almost as soon as the movie had begun. Also, his ankle still really hurt. There were definitely pluses and minuses to having a broken bone.

When Sammy and David and Dad went to work on the raft, Buddy trotted out into the yard with them. But Champ stayed put, as close to Charles as he could get. When Charles leaned down to scratch between his ears, the skinny dog gazed up at him with sparkling golden-brown eyes. His wagging tail thumped on the deck.

I'm keeping a close eye on you, my friend. We don't want you getting hurt again.

"Aunt Amanda liked you," Charles said to Champ. "She said you had a lot of potential, even though you don't look so great right now."

Charles's aunt had stopped by earlier to bring some books and magazines for Charles to read as he rested. Most of them were about dogs, since Aunt Amanda was even crazier about dogs than

Lizzie was. She even ran a doggy day-care center and had four dogs of her own.

Reggie had called to say he wanted to stop by, too. "Gotta check up on that pup," he'd said. "Gotta make sure you're taking good care of him."

Now Charles watched as his friends hammered and sawed. The raft was really coming together, right in front of his eyes. Charles couldn't believe that he was not going to be able to ride on it as it raced down the river. He just knew it would be a winner, with its three tall masts and bright red sails. Mom was planning to dye some old sheets for them to use, and Charles was hoping he'd be able to help paint their Viking logo — a hat with horns — when the time came. Charles was practicing in a notebook, trying to get the design right, as he lay on the lounge chair.

He saw Champ sit up suddenly and sniff the

air. His eyes were bright and his ears were pricked high, on alert.

Somebody's here. And I think I know who it is!

"Anybody home?" Reggie appeared around the corner of the house. "Hey, bud," he said as soon as he saw Champ. "Come here!"

Champ stood up but didn't move. He looked at Charles.

Okay with you?

Charles laughed. "Go on," he said.

Champ charged down the deck stairs and dashed toward his friend. Reggie knelt and opened his arms. "Hey, pal," he said. "Hey, there."

"Huh. He sure did bond with you," someone said.

That was when Charles realized that Reggie was not alone. He had brought Sarge with him! The big man smiled, walked up onto the deck, and handed Charles a stack of comic books. "I always liked looking at these when I was your age and feeling poorly," he said as he pulled up a chair and sat down next to Charles.

"Thanks," said Charles.

Sarge looked out at the backyard. "What the heck is that, Peterson?" he asked. "You don't think that thing is actually going to float, do you?"

Aha. Now Charles understood. Sarge and Reggie might have come to see him — but they were also on a mission. They were there to check out the competition.

"It'll do more than float," Dad called back. "It's going to be the fastest raft that river has ever seen."

Reggie and Champ walked up onto the deck. "He's gaining weight already," Reggie said. "And his coat is shinier. All he needed was a little care." He turned to Sarge. "I'm telling you, this dog could be a K-9 patroller. Did you hear? He has a natural alert. He ran to the back door and barked when Charles got hurt."

"What's an alert?" Charles asked.

"It's when a dog lets you know that something needs attention," Sarge said. "If he smells a lost person, for example. Or finds drugs, or explosives. Some dogs are trained to just sit quietly when that happens, and other dogs learn to bark and whine."

Sarge looked down at Champ and shook his head. "But I doubt that's what he was doing. He was probably just excited. He's been cooped up in that house full of animals all his life — anything new must seem exciting to him. It was just a coincidence that he barked when you got hurt." He reached down and scratched Champ's ears. "I'm sure he'll make somebody a good pet. He's obviously a sweet guy. But I wouldn't take him into my program, no way. A dog that grew up the way he did is just too damaged."

Reggie shrugged. "Have it your way," he said. "I still think you're missing out."

"If you want to see some of our K-9 teams in action, you're welcome to come to one of our trainings," Sarge said to Charles. "Something to do while you're sitting around, healing up."

Charles nodded eagerly. "Definitely!" he said. "I'd love to."

"I'll arrange it with your dad," said Sarge, getting up to leave. "Let's hit the road, Reggie. I've got paperwork waiting back at the station."

Reggie said good-bye to Charles and gave Champ one more pat. "See you soon, pooch," he said. "Good luck with that raft," he called to Dad as he left. "You'll need it."

As the day wore on, Charles grew bored. It was no fun sitting on the deck while his friends worked on the raft. It was even less fun sitting there staring at the partly finished raft after they'd said good-bye and left for the day. Dad said he would help Charles inside, but first he packed up the tools and went to stow them in the basement.

Charles waited and waited, but Dad didn't come back out. Finally, he couldn't stand it anymore. He had to get a closer look at the way they had attached the masts. Were they really going to hold? Anyway, he needed practice on his crutches, didn't he? He hauled himself out of the chair, grabbed his crutches, and began to pick his way down the deck stairs.

Champ paced and whimpered.

Not a good idea! Wait! Don't do it.

"I'm fine, you worrywart," Charles said, turning to smile at the dog. That was when his crutch slipped and he went *thumpthumpthump* down the rest of the steps.

CHAPTER EIGHT

"Now we know it wasn't just a coincidence," Charles said to his dad. "Will you tell Sarge what happened?"

They were on their way to watch the K-9 teams' training, a few days after Charles's second tumble. Charles wanted Sarge to hear all about how Champ had barked and barked until Dad had run out to help Charles up from where he'd fallen. Fortunately, Charles had not hurt his leg — but the important thing was that Champ had "alerted" again; Charles was sure of it.

"I'll tell him," Dad said. "But I think his mind is made up about that dog."

"I know," said Charles. "But mine is, too. I know Champ has what it takes to be a K-9 patroller. Can't we try to convince Sarge?"

Charles had hated to say good-bye to Champ, even though it was just for the afternoon, but he was looking forward to this special time with Dad. By now he'd had his permanent cast put on — bright neon green, his favorite color — and he had gotten better at getting around on crutches, but Mom insisted he still wasn't quite ready to go back to school. This visit to the K-9 training center was coming just in time, before Charles died of boredom.

Dad pulled into a complex of brick buildings with wide green lawns between them. "This is the police academy," Dad said. "Firefighters do some training here, too. There's a building here we can set on fire, for practice."

"Cool," said Charles, but he was barely listening.

His eyes were on the dogs. As they pulled into a parking spot, he saw a cluster of men and women standing near a police cruiser. They weren't in uniform, but most of them wore T-shirts that said POLICE or mentioned the city or town where they worked. At their sides were some of the most beautiful dogs Charles had ever seen. "Wow," he said. "I can see why Sarge thinks Champ is scrawny." These dogs, mostly German shepherds, were fit and muscular, like superheroes. Their coats gleamed, and everything about them said "ready for action."

A tall man strode over to introduce himself as they got out of the pickup. "Lieutenant Tim Oliver," he said, shaking hands with Dad, then Charles. "You can call me Tim. I'm the head trainer for our state's K-9 units. Sarge got called away on an emergency, but he told me you'd be coming." He motioned for Charles and Dad to follow him, and walked slowly so that Charles could keep up on his crutches. "We're doing recertifications today," he said. "These officers and their dogs have trained for years and passed all kinds of tests to become K-9 teams, but they still have to come here once a year and show us their stuff." He introduced Charles and his dad to the officers, explaining that they were friends of Sarge's who had come to observe.

"Can I say hi to the dogs?" Charles asked.

"As long as the handler says it's okay," said Tim. "But stay out of their way when they're working. They need to focus." He looked down at a clipboard. "We're going to start with some basic obedience testing," he said. "I've set up a spot for you to sit, over there." He pointed to a cluster of lawn chairs at one end of a wide green lawn. Charles and Dad headed for the seats, and Dad helped Charles put his foot up on one of the extra chairs.

Tim called each of the officers in order, and Dad and Charles watched as they put their dogs through their paces. The dogs heeled at their sides, sticking like glue no matter what speed the handlers went or how many turns they took. They stayed put when their handlers told them to stay and galloped toward them eagerly when they called, "Come."

Most impressive of all was at the end of the test, when the handlers told their dogs, "Down, stay!" then went off to hide out of sight for five whole minutes.

Clipboard in hand, Tim strolled over to talk to Charles and Dad while one of the dogs was lying still, waiting to be released from his stay.

"Watch this," he said. He stepped forward and whistled loudly, fingers between his teeth. "Come, Arrow! Here, boy! Want your ball?"

Charles didn't think that was very fair. What dog could resist a whistle and a ball? He was sure Arrow would break out of his stay, even though he wasn't supposed to pay attention to anyone but his handler, Jason.

But the dog, a gleaming black German shepherd, did not twitch an ear. He ignored Tim and lay as still as a statue, waiting to hear Jason's voice. Moments later, when the time was up and Jason called his name, Arrow leapt to his feet and dashed straight for his handler. "Good boy!" said Jason. He flipped a tennis ball into the air, and Arrow jumped to catch it.

"These dogs and handlers are partners in the truest sense of the word," Tim told Dad and Charles. "They are together 24-7, every hour of the day. The dogs live with their partners, train with them, work with them, and protect them until the dogs get old and have to retire. Then they live out the rest of their days as pets, still with their partners."

"How old are the dogs when they start training?" Charles asked.

"They can be as young as six months," said Tim. "Arrow there, he was almost a year old. He was a rescue, a dog who nobody knew how to handle. He wasn't treated well by his first owner, and he got a little out of hand. Jason came along just in time. He saw Arrow's potential and guessed that all he needed was a job. Sure enough, now they're one of the best teams in the state."

Charles felt tears come to his eyes. What a great story!

Jason and Arrow came to check on what they were supposed to do next, and Charles asked if he could pet the dog. "Sure," said Jason. Arrow still had the slobbery green tennis ball in his mouth.

"That's his favorite toy," Jason said. "He'd rather have that as a reward than any treat." He looked down fondly at his dog.

After the obedience testing, Charles and Dad drove to another field, where an agility course was set up. This one was nothing like the brightly painted agility courses Charles had seen. Instead, there were high walls for the dogs to scramble up, walkways made of chicken wire that would be hard on a dog's feet, rusted drainpipes to squeeze through, and barrels to leap over. "These dogs really are superheroes," Charles said to Dad as they watched a dog named Mozart race around the course, following the directions of his owner, Tyler.

After that, the dogs went through their other tests, showing how they could sniff for drugs and explosives; help their partners at a "traffic stop," where an officer in a police car pulled over another officer pretending to be a speeder; and jump on a "bad guy" and latch on with their teeth (the pretend bad guy, another officer, was wearing a thick cuff over his arm for the dog to bite into) until their handlers told them to let go.

Charles watched in awe as a muscular black-and-tan dog ran at the "bad guy" so fast that he was nothing but a blur. His handler, Rich, said that the dog's name was Drager, and that he was the fastest, strongest dog in the state.

"Is he a German shepherd?" Charles asked as he petted Drager with Rich's permission.

Rich shook his head. "He's a Belgian Malinois. They're a type of shepherd that is perfect for police or military use, because they're so smart and strong." He grinned. "They can be a handful, too. If I don't keep Drager busy at all times, he'll destroy my house."

Charles was so interested that he nearly forgot about his broken ankle. All afternoon as he watched the dogs go through their paces, Charles could not stop thinking about how much Champ would love this job. There had to be some way to convince Sarge that the scrawny pup could turn into a superhero, too.

CHAPTER NINE

"Where's Daddy? When is Daddy's boat coming?" The Bean bounced up and down with excitement.

It was the day of the raft race. Almost a week had gone by since Charles's visit to the training center, and a lot had changed since then. Charles's cast was more of a muddy green by now, covered with signatures and drawings by friends and family. His armpits were sore from walking with crutches, but he could handle stairs with ease and his ankle hardly hurt anymore. Champ's coat was even shinier, he had gained more weight, and Lizzie and Charles had already taught him to sit, shake hands, sit pretty, and — best of all — "take!"

(pick up) and "bring!" (deliver) objects to someone (usually Charles) who needed them. And finally, the Viking raft had been finished and driven to the race site on a borrowed trailer, with red sails proudly raised.

It had not been easy for Charles to watch his dad and his two best friends get the raft ready to launch that morning at the starting line. They laughed and joked in their horned Viking helmets as they made sure that no nails had popped out and the raft was ready to race. "Wish you could come with us," David said to Charles.

"Me too," Charles said. But he knew it was better this way: with his broken ankle he'd only be in the way, and there was a good chance his cast could get wet. He looked around at the other rafts scattered along the shoreline, ready to be put into the water. "I don't see any boat here that can beat ours."

Sammy smiled and pushed his Viking helmet

back to get a better look. "There are some funny ones, though," he said. "Did you see the one with hula dancers on it?" He pointed to a beach-scene raft surrounded by people wearing grass skirts. They were loading up their water guns, getting ready to blast the competition and the crowds that would line the course. Another raft had a disco theme, with dancers in sparkly outfits and a boom box thumping out music.

Some rafts were fancy, with old barrels for flotation or special steering devices. Others were patched-together messes created from swimming noodles, duct tape, and inner tubes. Some would make it to the finish line, but others would probably self-destruct before the race ended. Dad nudged Charles and pointed out a lumpy, crooked raft made of air mattresses roped together. "That's Reggie's raft," he said. "I'd say he's better at hitting a softball than building boats, wouldn't you?"

Charles laughed and waved at Reggie. "Good luck!" he called. "Champ and I will be watching for you!"

Now Charles was sitting with Mom, Lizzie, the Bean, and all the spectators on the riverbank near the finish line. The crowd buzzed with excitement as they waited for the first rafts to appear.

Charles looked down at the dog by his side. They had brought Champ along — since Lizzie said it was good for him to get used to all types of situations and people. Mom had hitched his leash to Charles's chair, even though it was very unlikely that he would run off. Champ had stuck to Charles like glue all week, barely leaving his side and whimpering at the door when Charles said good-bye on the day he went back to school.

Can't I come with you? What if something happens? I need to be there.

"Daddy's boat will come soon," Charles told the Bean now. "I bet it will be the first one we see." He imagined himself standing tall in his Viking helmet as their red-sailed raft cruised to an easy win and the firefighters evened the score with their police rivals.

"The current is strong," Lizzie said. "Look at those kayakers. They're having trouble paddling upstream."

She pointed to two women, one in a bright blue boat and one in a yellow boat, who paddled furiously but barely moved.

"That must be because of the rain last night," Mom said. "The river is high. Good thing we have nice weather today for the race."

Charles looked around at the crowd. He recognized a lot of faces: many of the police officers who had been at the softball game were there, along with their families. Charles waved to Meg, who was sitting with some of the other firefighters. "Go, Vikings!" he called to her, and she smiled and gave him a thumbs-up. Then he saw a big man standing near the finish line. Even from the back, he could tell who it was. "There's Sarge," he said, pointing him out to Lizzie.

"Wait till he sees Champ now," Lizzie said. "He'll have to be impressed."

Charles wondered if he should take a little walk so that Sarge could see how carefully Champ would stay by his side, watching Charles's every move. But before Charles even reached for his crutches, Champ sprang to his feet. His eyes were bright and focused upstream, and his big ears swiveled this way and that as he listened.

Charles strained his own ears but couldn't hear anything except the faint sound of dance music. Was the disco float ahead of Dad's boat?

Suddenly, Champ lunged forward. His leash,

still tied to Charles's chair, grew taut and then snapped — but not before Charles was thrown out of the chair and onto the ground. "Hey!" he said as Champ dashed toward the river, so fast he was almost a blur.

"Honey, are you all right?" Mom asked as she rushed to help Charles up. "I can't believe he did that."

Charles brushed off his pants. He was fine but shaken. He had trusted Champ to take care of him. Why had the dog just run off like that? Maybe Sarge was right about Champ after all. Maybe he just wasn't cut out to be a hero.

CHAPTER TEN

"I'll go catch Champ," said Lizzie. She unhooked the broken leash from Charles's chair. "He didn't mean to hurt you. I think he heard something. Like maybe somebody needs help." She ran off toward the river.

Mom helped Charles get settled back on his chair. "Is your leg okay?" she asked. "Did you bump it when you fell? What about your head? Did you hit your head?"

"I'm fine — really." Charles craned his neck, trying so see around his mother. "What's going on down there, anyway?"

Mom turned to look. "Isn't that your Viking raft?" she asked. "Look! It's in first place." She paused. "But — wait. What's that?"

Charles hopped up onto his crutches so he could see. "That's a raft, too," he said. "It's Reggie's ridiculous raft — and it's sinking."

Now, over the sound of Champ's barking, he could hear Reggie shouting for help. "Grab the rope!" he was yelling. "Grab it!" Charles saw Reggie toss a heavy rope toward shore, but it fell short of the riverbank. Desperately, he reeled it in to try again.

Reggie's raft was in trouble.

The roped-together air mattresses were seriously sagging, the raft was spinning around so that it was floating backward, sideways, and every which way, and Reggie was holding on for dear life. At that spot in the river, the current was too fast for even a strong swimmer to be safe. Even though he was wearing a life vest like all the other racers, Reggie needed help. The water was cold and the current was wild.

Charles heard Dad yell, "Hard to starboard!" to Sammy and David. Both boys dug in with their oars, paddling as hard as they could to turn their raft toward Reggie's. The red sails dipped and swayed, and for a moment Charles thought the raft might flip over, but all that happened was that Sammy's Viking hat fell off and floated away downstream.

Champ raced along the riverbank, following Reggie's raft as it slid rapidly past and barking as he galloped.

Need some help here! I can't do it alone! Come on, people!

"He must have heard Reggie's voice before any of us could," Charles said to his mom. He knew that dogs could hear much better than humans. "Lizzie was right. Champ knew something was wrong."

By now, other spectators had begun to run closer to the river. Charles had noticed that firefighters were always ready to help, even if it meant running into a dangerous situation. He could tell that the police were the same way.

Reggie tossed the rope toward shore again. "Help!" he yelled. "I'm sinking fast!"

As Lizzie drew closer to Champ, she called, "Champ! Take it! Take it!"

Without hesitation, Champ splashed into the water and grabbed the rope in his teeth. "Bring it!" Lizzie called, but Champ already knew what to do. He turned and scrabbled back up onto shore, carrying the rope in his teeth. Eager hands reached out to grab it. The police and firefighters worked together, like a tug-of-war team, and soon the raft had been hauled halfway onto the riverbank. Reggie rolled off onto the ground, then stood and shook himself. "I'm okay," Reggie said. "Phew. Thanks, guys." Champ pushed through the crowd to run to Reggie's side. "Yes, that includes you, of course," Reggie said. He stooped down to ruffle Champ's ears. "You most of all, pal. You saved me."

Charles felt a pang of jealousy, but at the same time he was so proud of Champ that he almost felt like crying. Champ *was* a hero. There was no question about it now. Charles would always know it was true, even if nobody else did.

Meanwhile, the Viking raft had spun around and crashed into the riverbank, screeching to a halt as five or six other rafts, including the Hawaiian-themed one, coasted by to loud cheers from the spectators.

Dad, Sammy, and David hopped off the raft and scampered to a safe perch onshore. "Wow, that river is really running today! I've never seen it like that before." Dad said.

"You would have won," Charles said. "You were way out in front." He crutched his way over to give Dad a hug. "But it was better that you came to help Reggie." It was true. Suddenly, winning the raft race didn't seem important at all.

Dad went to shake hands with Reggie. "Glad you're okay," he said. "That water is cold. I think we have an extra blanket over by our chairs."

"Yeah, my partner's shivering a little bit," Reggie said, looking down at Champ.

"I meant for you — Hey, wait, did you say 'partner'?" Dad asked.

Reggie nodded. "Surprise! Big news. I was waiting till after the race to tell you, but I finally talked Sarge into at least trying Champ in the K-9 program. He agreed after he heard about Champ's second natural alert, when you fell down the stairs." He smiled at Charles. "Your dad told me about that. I was so proud of Champ, and now I'm even prouder. I know he's going to be a star."

"But what about that 'partner' part?" Charles asked.

"Oh, right," said Reggie. "Well, part of the deal was that I would join the program, too. It didn't take much to convince me, if I knew I could work with this guy. We're going to be a K-9 team! I already found a new place to rent. It's even cheaper than my old place, and I can have a dog there." He thumped Champ's side, and Champ grinned up at him and held up a paw.

Partners. Forever.

Just then, Sarge pushed through the crowd. "How're my latest recruits?" he said. "No major injuries? Good. Nice work, Champ. We start training on Monday, at oh eight hundred." He gave Reggie a salute, ruffled Champ's ears, nodded to Charles and his dad, and headed off. Before he turned away, Charles saw a smile on the gruff man's face.

Charles was smiling, too. This was the best day ever, even if the Viking raft had not won the race. Champ had proved he was a superhero after all, and now he had found the perfect home — and partner.

PUPPY TIPS

Sadly, hoarding cases like the one Champ came from are not uncommon. Some people really get carried away by their love of animals and try to take care of too many at once. Thirty or forty dogs is probably more than anyone can handle! When the police and the humane society discover these cases, the animals are rescued and new homes are found for them. Years ago my brother's family adopted one of these dogs, a beagle mix named Lucy, and she had a very happy life with them.

Dear Reader,

When I was working on this book, I was able to watch some K-9 teams in action as they trained at the Vermont Police Academy in Pittsford. (One of the best parts of being a writer is that I get to do research like this!) I was near tears all day as I watched the dogs showing off what they could do. I was amazed at how well the dogs were trained, and I was very moved by the strong and beautiful bond they had with their handlers. These teams work so hard together and obviously have a great time as well. When I went home, I rewrote a whole section of my book so that I could include what I had seen, showing it through Charles's eyes. Many thanks to Lieutenant Tim Oliver, Jason and Arrow, Tyler and Mozart, Rich and Drager, and all the other teams I watched that day.

After my visit, I donated to a charity called Lacey's Fund, which helps K-9 police afford veterinarian care for their retired and aging partners. In many states, there are also funds set up to buy bulletproof vests to protect K-9 patrol dogs. It's a good feeling to help these teams, who work so hard to help and protect us.

Yours from the Puppy Place,

Ellen Miles

P.S. For books about some other dog heroes, check out SCOUT and MUTTLEY.

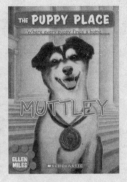

ABOUT THE AUTHOR

Ellen Miles loves dogs, which is why she has a great time writing the Puppy Place books. And guess what? She loves cats, too! (In fact, her very first pet was a beautiful tortoiseshell cat named Jenny.) That's why she came up with the Kitty Corner series. Ellen lives in Vermont and loves to be outdoors with her dog, Zipper, every day, walking, biking, skiing, or swimming, depending on the season. She also loves to read, cook, explore her beautiful state, play with dogs, and hang out with friends and family.

Visit Ellen at www.ellenmiles.net.

LET THE GAME BEGIN!

SEE WHERE IT ALL STARTED IN
BOOK #1!

Puppy Powers

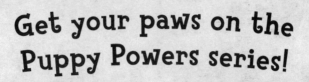

We'll be there in a whisker!

Dr. KittyCat is a talented vet—and an adorable cat. She takes purr-fect care of all her patients!